PASS THE ROCK

PASS THE ROCK

Transform the Game

RICHARD HEMPHILL, JR.

Printed in the United States of America
Keen Vision Publishing, LLC
www.publishwithkvp.com
ISBN: 978-1-948270-94-6

FOR THE BIGGEST GIANT SLAYER I KNOW, MY WIFE, IRMANIE
HEMPHILL, MD, FAAFP, AND MY SON, RICHARD HEMPHILL,
III

A WORD FROM THE AUTHOR

LADIES AND GENTLEMAN, BOYS AND GIRLS, CHILDREN OF ALL AGES, YOU HAVE JUST ENTERED THE MOST EXCITING ARENA OF SPORTS THE WORLD HAS EVER SEEN: THE DUGOUT. THE ATHLETES YOU WILL MEET IN <u>THE DUGOUT SERIES</u> DO NOT PLAY FOR A TROPHY, THEY STRIVE FOR THE CROWN. IN HEAVEN, THE CROWD IS GOING WILD THAT YOU ARE HERE TO WITNESS THE GREATEST GAMES EVER PLAYED.

FACING ETERNITY, I INVITE YOU TO STAND ON YOUR FEET, GET EXCITED AND WITNESS HOW THESE BIBLE ALL-STARS TRANSFORM THE GAME. EACH STORY IS PURPOSED FOR CHILDREN TO LEARN HOW TO BE BOLD, HAVE COURAGE, TRUST, AND BELIEVE IN THE SPORTS ARENA AND LIFE.

THE BEST NEWS IS THAT THE GAMES DO NOT STOP HERE. YOU TOO CAN JOIN TEAM DUGOUT: THE ONLY PLACE WHERE THE WORLD OF SPORTS, MEETS THE HALL OF FAITH.

GRAB A SNACK. MAKE SOME NOISE. TELL A FRIEND.

THE GAME IS ABOUT TO BEGIN!

MICHAEL THE ANNOUNCER:
"IT'S GAME DAY AT THE PROMISE LAND STADIUM,
AND WE ARE IN FOR A TREAT. THE SOCOH GIANTS
WILL TAKE ON ELAH VALLEY FOR THE CHAMPIONSHIP.
WE'RE YOUR ANNOUNCERS, MICHAEL & GABRIEL.
GABRIEL, WHO DO YOU THINK WILL WIN TODAY?"

GOLIATH OF GATH

SOCOH GIANTS

9'9 450 LBS

GABRIEL THE ANNOUNCER:

"I DON'T KNOW! THIS IS DEFINITELY GOING TO BE A TOUGH ONE. I MEAN, JUST LOOK AT GOLIATH OF GATH AKA G2 OF THE SOCOH GIANTS. HE IS BIG AND SCARY — ONE OF THE MOST DOMINANT PLAYERS WE HAVE EVER SEEN."

MICHAEL THE ANNOUNCER:
"YOU'RE RIGHT, IT WILL DEFINITELY BE A GAME TO WATCH.
ELAH VALLEY, LED BY COACH SAUL, HAVE SPENT THE LAST
40 GAMES TRYING TO GET OUT OF THE WILDERNESS AND THEY
BARELY MADE IT TO PROMISE LAND STADIUM TODAY. I AM
NOT TOO CONFIDENT THAT THEY ARE READY. GOD HAS TO BE
WITH THEM."

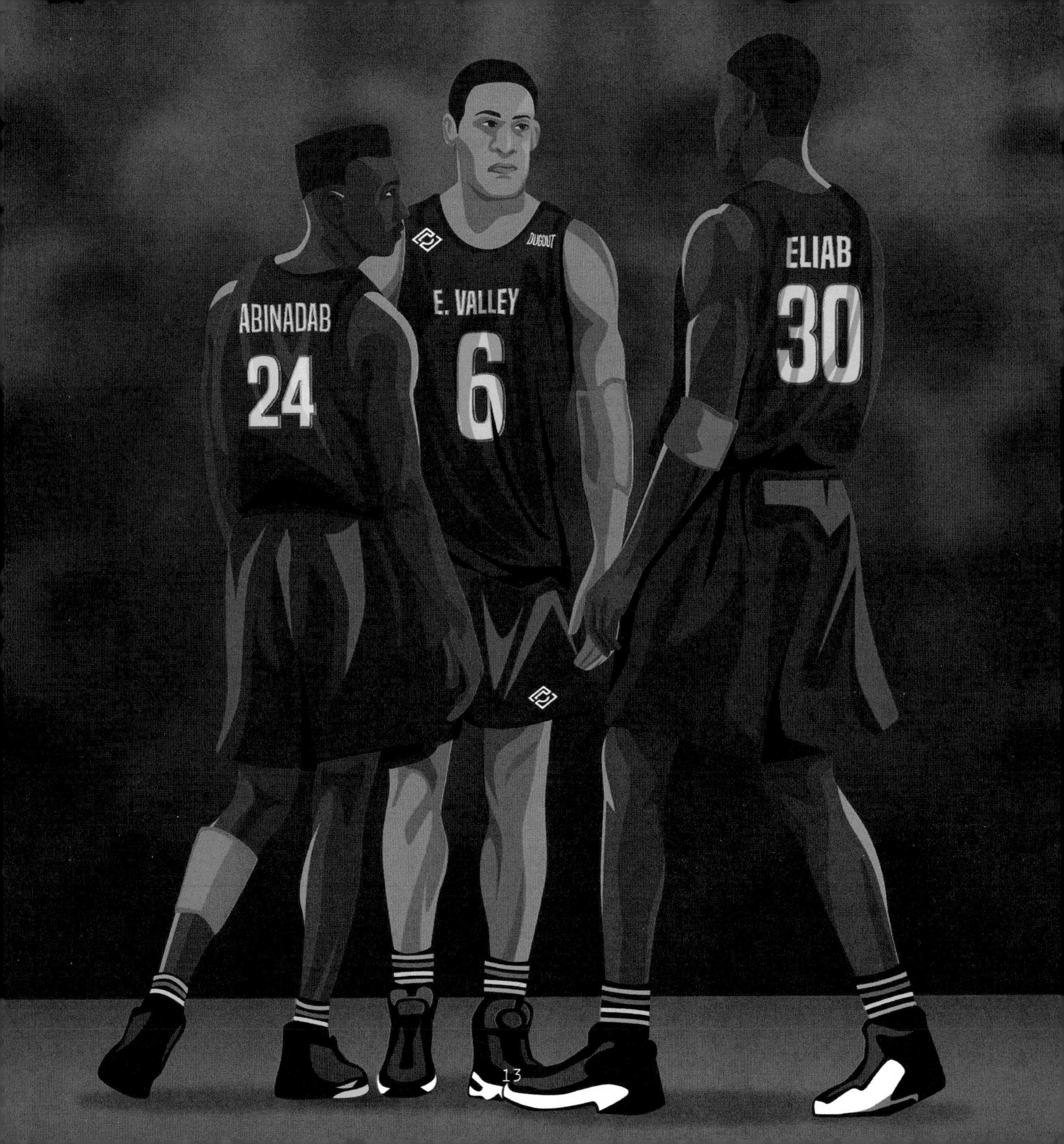

ABINADAB
24
DUGOUT
E. VALLEY
6
ELIAB
30

"WHY DID YOU EVEN SHOW UP? G2 WAS MADE FOR THIS MOMENT AND YOU ARE LED BY COACH SAUL. YOU ALL ARE PATHETIC." G2 SAYS TO ELAH VALLEY."IF YOU WANT THE CROWN, YOU WILL HAVE TO COME THROUGH ME."

GABRIEL THE ANNOUNCER:
"WELL, YOU HEARD G2. HE'S NOT WASTING ANYTIME GETTING INTO HIS OPPONENTS' HEADS. THE SOCOH GIANTS ARE CONFIDENT THAT THEY HAVE THE CHAMPIONSHIP IN THE BAG!"

"COACH SAUL, WE DO NOT STAND A CHANCE," ONE OF THE PLAYERS FROM ELAH VALLEY SAYS. "G2 IS BIGGER, STRONGER, FASTER, AND A PROVEN CHAMPION. HOW ARE WE GOING TO COMPETE WITH THAT? WE DO NOT HAVE ANYONE WHO CAN MATCHUP WITH HIM."

DUGOUT

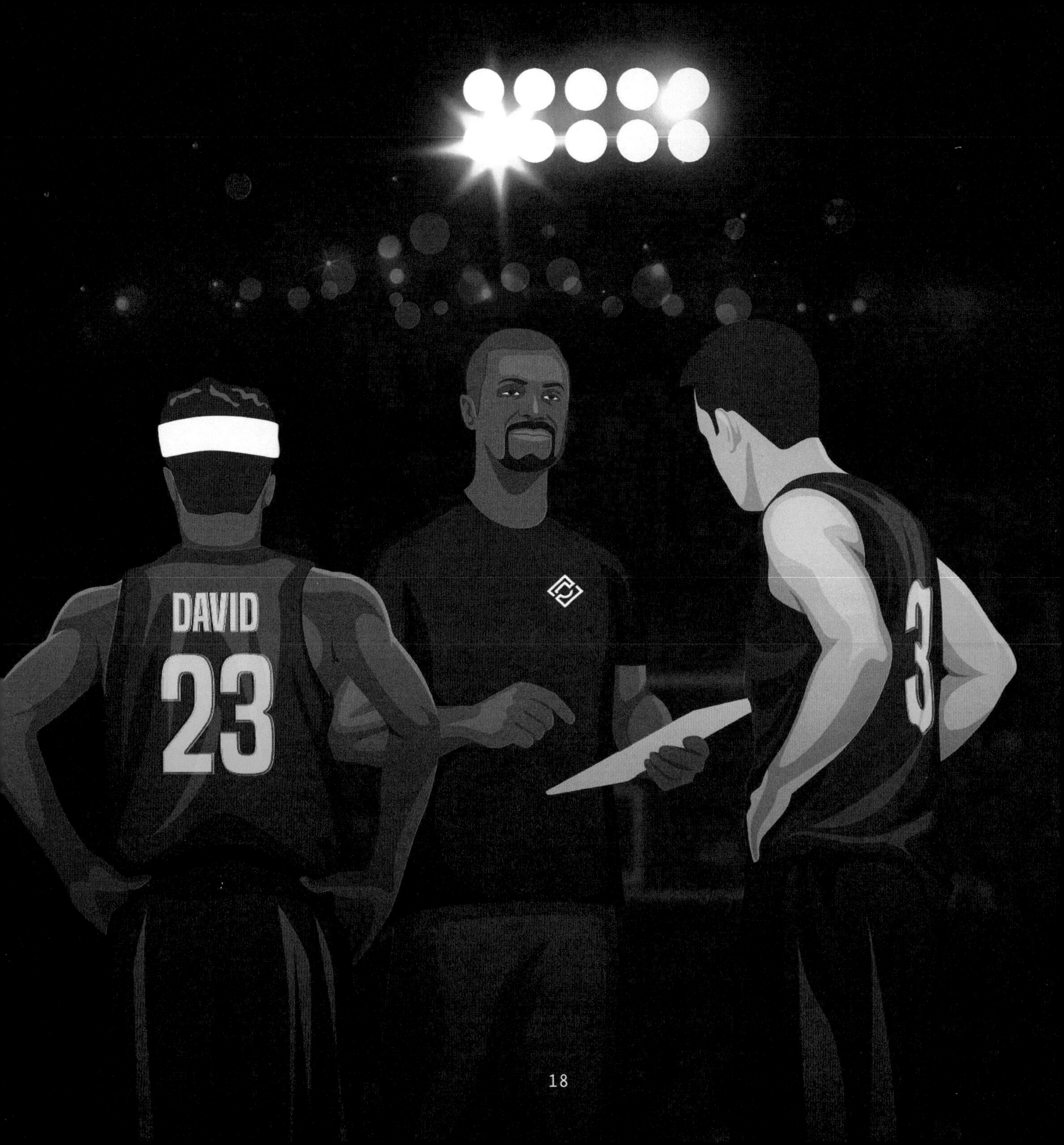
DAVID
23
3

"DON'T WORRY, LET'S JUST DO THE BEST WE CAN." COACH SAUL REPLIES. "GOD WILL HELP US. HE IS ALWAYS ON OUR SIDE. LET'S HUDDLE UP, TEAM. TRANSFORM ON THREE!"

1... 2... 3...TRANSFORM!

GABRIEL THE ANNOUNCER:
"OKAY, FOLKS. HERE'S THE TIPOFF. WITH ELAH VALLEY'S ROTATION DOWN TO EIGHT PLAYERS, THEY ARE REALLY GOING TO NEED ELIAB, ABINADAB, AND SHAMMAH TO STEP UP. I KNOW THEIR FATHER, JESSE, IS PROUD OF THEM, BUT THEIR SEASON ENDS TONIGHT."

MICHAEL THE ANNOUNCER:
"I DON'T KNOW. WE MAY BE IN FOR A SURPRISE. SOME WAY, SOME HOW, ELAH VALLEY ALWAYS SEEMS TO PULL THROUGH. LET'S SEE WHAT HAPPENS TONIGHT!"

GABRIEL THE ANNOUNCER:
"AND WE'RE OFF TO A FAST START. G2 DRIBBLES TO THE LEFT, DRIBBLES TO THE RIGHT AND BOOM-SHAKA-LAKA! THAT WAS TOO EASY! DO YOU SEE WHAT I'M SAYING, MICHAEL? THE SOCOH GIANTS ARE TAKING THE CROWN HOME TONIGHT!"

"TIMEOUT!" SHOUTS COACH SAUL. "DAVID, BRING THE BOYS SOME WATER NOW."

ONCE THE TEAM GATHERS TOGETHER, COACH SAUL GIVES THEM A QUICK PEP TALK AS THEY DRINK THEIR WATER.

"LISTEN, TEAM. GOD HAS NOT GIVEN YOU A SPIRIT OF FEAR BUT OF POWER, LOVE, AND A SOUND MIND. NOW GET OUT THERE AND DOMINATE!"

ELAH VALLEY HEADS DOWN THE COURT. SHARP PASS TO ABINADAB, HE SHOOTS AND...

G2 SENDS IT INTO THE STANDS!

GABRIEL THE ANNOUNCER:
"WELL, FOLKS, IT DOESN'T LOOK LIKE THAT QUICK TIMEOUT FROM COACH SAUL HELPED A BIT. ELAH VALLEY DOES NOT BELIEVE A WORD COACH SAUL SAID TO THEM. THEY HAVE TO BELIEVE IF THEY ARE GOING TO WIN THIS CHAMPIONSHIP.

MICHAEL THE ANNOUNCER:
"I AGREE, GABRIEL. RIGHT NOW, ELAH VALLEY IS PLAYING AS IF THEY HAVE ALREADY LOST. THEY'RE GOING TO NEED A LITTLE MORE FAITH IF THEY WANT TO WIN THIS GAME.

"IF THEY WOULD JUST PUT ME IN THE GAME AND PASS ME THE ROCK, WE WOULD DEFEAT THIS TEAM AND G2," DAVID SAYS. DAVID WAS THE YOUNGEST PLAYER ON THE TEAM AND HE NEVER GOT ANY PLAYING TIME. THEY ONLY LET HIM BRING THE TEAM WATER AND FRESH TOWELS.

"JUST BECAUSE I'M YOUNG DOES NOT MEAN I CAN'T HELP THEM WIN!" DAVID SAYS TO HIMSELF.

DAVID DECIDES TO TELL COACH SAUL HOW HE FEELS.

28

"LISTEN, DAVID," COACH SAUL SAYS. "I HEAR YOU, BUT YOU ARE NOT READY FOR THIS STAGE. G2 HAS DOMINATED ON THIS STAGE SINCE HE WAS A LITTLE BOY. HE WILL PROBABLY GO DOWN AS THE GREATEST PLAYER IN THE HALL OF FAME."

"THAT'S WHERE YOU ARE WRONG," DAVID REPLIES. "I AM READY. I HAVE DEFEATED OPPONENTS AS FIERCE AS LIONS AND AS STRONG AS BEARS. GIVE ME A CHANCE AND YOU'LL SEE!"

"OKAY, DAVID. SUIT UP. I'M GOING TO PUT YOU IN THE GAME," COACH SAUL FINALLY GIVES IN.

DAVID DRESSES QUICKLY AND RUNS TO THE COURT.

As david walks onto the court, G2 starts laughing. "Is this your plan to beat me? A tiny boy? Give me the championship crown now." G2 says to elah valley.

David stares at G2 and says loudly, "I'm David from Elah Valley, and I'm going to show you just who I am! Who are you?"

The crowd chants, "Who are you? Who are you? Who are you?"

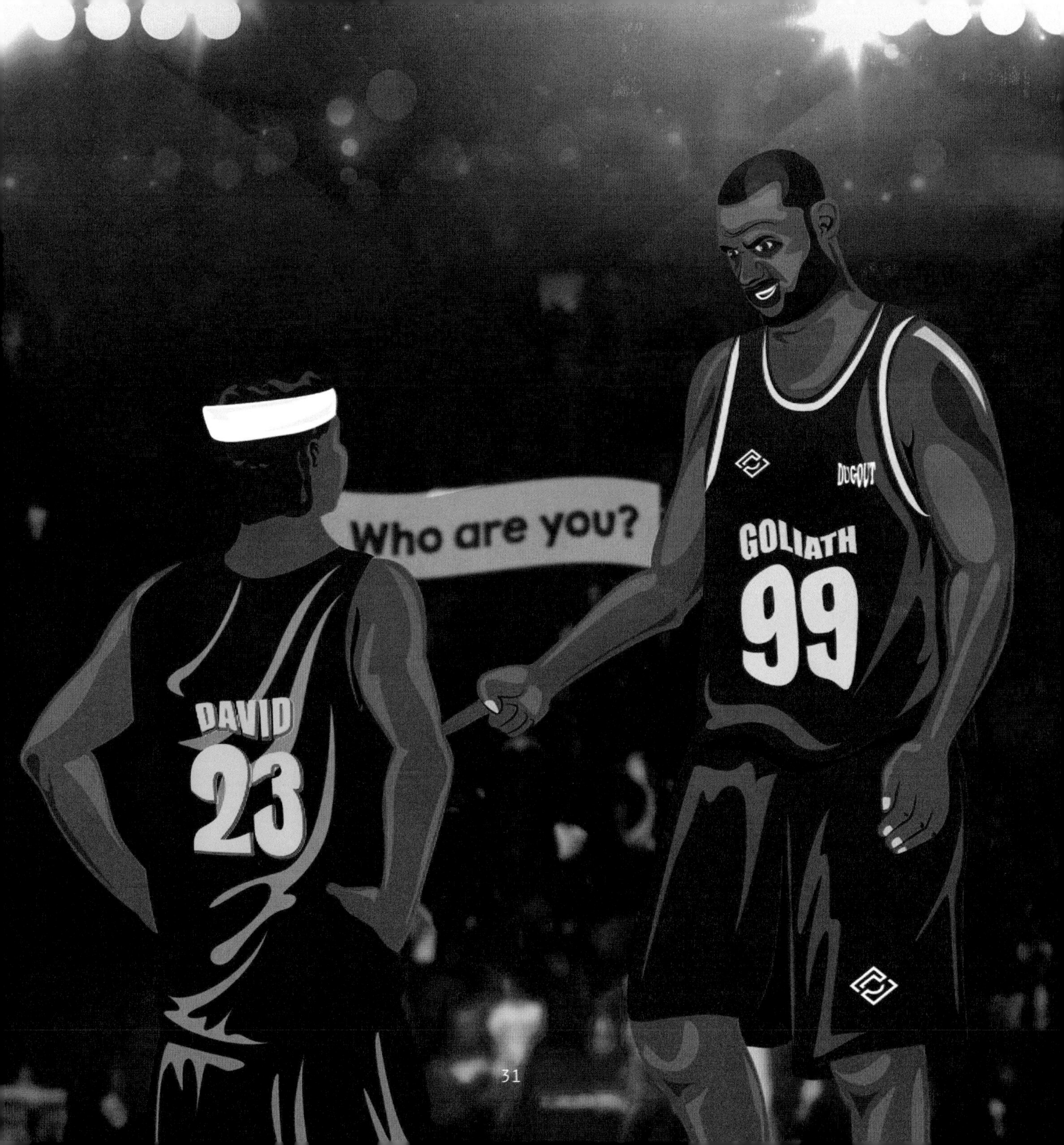
Who are you?
DUGOUT
GOLIATH
99
DAVID
23

GABRIEL THE ANNOUNCER:

"WHAT'S GOING ON HERE? WITH YOUNG DAVID ON THE COURT, THINGS HAVE DEFINITELY TURNED AROUND FOR ELAH VALLEY. THEY ARE FINALLY CATCHING UP WITH THE SOCOH GIANTS. DO YOU THINK THEY CAN ACTUALLY WIN THIS, MICHAEL?"

MICHAEL THE ANNOUNCER:

"WELL, GABRIEL, THE SOCOH GIANTS LED THIS GAME FOR THE FIRST THREE QUARTERS, BUT IT'S ALL ABOUT WHO IS IN THE LEAD WHEN THE BUZZER SOUNDS. THE CROWD SEEMS TO BELIEVE THAT ELAH VALLEY WILL PULL THROUGH. WITHOUT THE ENERGY FROM THE CROWD, I DON'T KNOW IF SOCOH'S VICTORY WILL BE SO EASY ANYMORE."

GABRIEL THE ANNOUNCER:

"I AGREE, MICHAEL. TAKE A LOOK AT HOW YOUNG DAVID PLAYS! HE'S SMALL IN SIZE, BUT HE IS CONFIDENT IN WHO HE IS AND WHOSE HE IS. THAT MAY BE JUST THE THING ELAH VALLEY NEEDS TO WIN THIS CHAMPIONSHIP. COACH SAUL WILL DEFINITELY WANT TO KEEP THIS YOUNG MAN AROUND."

THE CROWD IS GOING CRAZY! WITH ONE-MINUTE LEFT, COACH SAUL CALLS FOR A TIMEOUT.

DAVID GATHERS THE TEAM AROUND FOR A PEP TALK. "LISTEN, TEAM, THIS IS WHERE WE TRANSFORM THE GAME. ON THE NEXT PLAY DOWN, G2 IS GOING TO TRY AND STEAL, KILL, AND DESTROY OUR HOPES AND DREAMS.
PASS ME THE ROCK!"

"YOU HEARD HIM, TEAM! PASS DAVID THE ROCK!" COACH SAUL REPLIES. "TRANSFORM ON 3!"

1...2...3...TRANSFORM!

36

GABRIEL THE ANNOUNCER:

"WE'RE HERE, IT'S THE FINAL MOMENT. ELAH VALLEY IS DOWN BY TWO AND THERE ARE 58 SECONDS LEFT ON THE CLOCK. CAN ELAH VALLEY DO THIS? WILL THEY TAKE HOME THE CHAMPIONSHIP?"

MICHAEL THE ANNOUNCER:

"DAVID TAKES THE INBOUND PASS, THROWS IT UP AHEAD TO ABINADAB. ABINADAB SPINS TO THE LEFT AND PASSES TO SHAMMAH. SHAMMAH SEES DAVID IN THE CORNER WIDE OPEN. G2 ANTICIPATES THE PASS AND GOES FOR THE STEAL. DAVID PULLS THE ROCK AWAY AND WITH FIVE SECONDS LEFT, DAVID SHOOTS THE ROCK OVER G2'S HEAD.

THE ENTIRE PROMISE LAND STADIUM IS SILENT AS THE ROCK SAILS THROUGH THE AIR.

NOTHING BUT NET! ELAH VALLEY AND THE CROWDS GO
WILD! DAVID HAS WON THE GAME.

GABRIEL THE ANNOUNCER:
"I CAN'T BELIEVE THIS! DAVID AND ELAH VALLEY HAVE
DEFEATED G2 AND THE SOCOH GIANTS. ELAH VALLEY HAS
WON THE CHAMPIONSHIP! WELL, MICHAEL, I GUESS GOD
WAS WITH THEM TODAY."

MICHAEL THE ANNOUNCER:
"DIDN'T YOU KNOW? GOD IS ALWAYS WITH THEM. AND WITH
FAITH AND GOD ON THEIR SIDE, THEY CAN DEFEAT ANY
OPPONENT THAT COMES THEIR WAY."

IS YOUR HEAD IN THE GAME?

Are you ready to test your skills?
Check your answers on page 42.

1. G2 IS FROM _____.
   A. GREENSBORO
   B. GREENWOOD
   C. GATH

2. DAVID AND HIS TEAM TRAINED IN _____.
   A. ELLENWOOD
   B. ELAH VALLEY
   C. ELMO'S HOUSE

3. ELAH VALLEY IS COACHED BY _____.
   A. COACH SAUL
   B. ARCH ANNOUNCER GABRIEL
   C. ARCH ANNOUNCER MICHAEL

4. WHAT WERE 2 OF DAVID'S TEAMMATES' NAMES?
   A. SHAQ & KOBE
   B. SHAMMAH & ABINIDAB
   C. LEBRON & D.WADE

5. ON PAGE 23, WHAT SCRIPTURE DID COACH SAUL QUOTE?
   A. 1 CORINTHIANS 12:1
   B. GALATIANS 6:9
   C. 2 TIMOTHY 1:7

6. IN ORDER TO WIN, ELAH VALLEY HAD TO HAVE _____.
   A. FAST RUNNERS
   B. DOPE FAKE PASSES
   C. FAITH

7. WHO SHOT THE WINNING SHOT TO WIN THE GAME?
   A. G2
   B. DAVID
   C. ABINIDAB

STAY CONNECTED

Author. Mentor. Sports Aficionado. Richard Hemphill Jr., founder of Team Dugout, embodies them all. The one-time collegiate-level basketball player turned sports mentor is on a mission to transform the game. In an era of countless stories involving the bad boys of sports, the "Transform the Game" series changes the sports arena from the inside out. Hemphill aims to raise a new generation of athletes with a heart for God and solid gold sportsmanlike character.

Thank you for reading, Pass the Rock. Richard looks forward to connecting with you. Here are a few ways you can connect with the author and stay updated on new releases, speaking engagements, products, and more.

FACEBOOK   The Dugout: Transform the Game Series
INSTAGRAM   transform_the_game_series
WEBSITE   www.t2gseries.com
EMAIL   transform@teamdugout.org

Made in the USA
Columbia, SC
06 June 2021